THIS BOOK
BELONGS TO

POST

This edition published by HarperCollins Publishers Ltd 1999 for Silverdale Books
An imprint of Bookmart Ltd
Registered Number 2372865
Trading as Bookmart Limited
Desford Rd, Enderby, Leicester, LE9 5AD
First published 1957 by Sampson Lowe
© Darrell Waters Limited 1957 as to all text and illustrations
Enid Blyton's signature mark and the word 'NODDY' are Registered
Trade Marks of Enid Blyton Ltd
All rights reserved
ISBN 0 26 167248-7
Printed and bound in Italy

DO LOOK OUT NODDY!

BY Enid Blyton

"I'LL PAY OUR TAXI-FARES WHEN WE GET BACK AGAIN,"
CRIED SALLY SKITTLE, HURRYING TO THE TRAIN

6

1. NODDY HAS AN IDEA

LITTLE Noddy woke up one morning with the sun shining on his face. He opened his eyes and blinked.

"Good gracious, sun, do go behind a cloud for a minute!" he said. "You're so bright I can hardly see. Oh, what a lovely day, I really must get up at once!" He jumped out of bed and sang loudly,

"The sun is shining
Up in the sky,
The birds are singing,
And so am I!

The bees are buzzing
As loud as can be,
The flowers are nodding
Their heads, like me!
The wind is blowing
The clouds along,
And I am singing
My little song!

"There!" said Noddy, putting on his red shirt. "I don't think even the blackbird could make up a song as quickly as that. I must remember to sing it to the milkman when he comes!"

"Milko! Milko!" sang the milkman coming up Noddy's path. "Oh, hallo, Noddy—you're up nice and early today. Let me tap your head to make it nod, then you won't need to pay for your milk this morning."

"No. I'll sing you my new song instead," said Noddy. "Listen! It just this minute came into my head."

So he sang it all over again and the milkman beat time with one of his milk bottles.

8

"Yes. That's worth a free bottle of milk," he said. "I don't know how you think of your songs, Noddy."

"I don't either," said Noddy. "I bet you are selling a lot of milk in this hot weather, aren't you Milkman?"

"No, I'm not," said the milkman, looking worried. "Most people in Toy Town have gone away on holiday now the weather is so fine."

"Yes, I know," said Noddy. "I've earned a lot of money taking people to the station. You see, I charge sixpence a person, and at least

9

twenty people have gone to the station in my little car."

"Ah—that's all very well!" said the milkman. "But with Toy Town half empty, what are you going to do when there's hardly anyone left to hire your car?"

"Dear me!" said Noddy, looking worried too. "I never thought of that! I was so pleased to take so many people to the station—and I've got lots more to take today—did you know that Sally Skittle and all her family are going to the seaside?"

"Yes, I did," said the milkman, looking so gloomy that Noddy felt quite alarmed. "Sally Skittle is one of my best customers, she has such a large family. And Miss Fluffy Cat has gone as well—and she usually has at least two bottles of milk a day."

"Well—I think *I* might go to the seaside too!" said Noddy, his head nodding up and down fast. "What a good idea! I shall go and tell my friend Big-Ears."

"Oh dear, if you go away and Big-Ears too—*and* his cat, I might as well give up my business," said the milkman. "*I* don't think that's a good idea of yours. But there—nobody thinks of the poor milkman when they shut up their houses and go away!"

And he went down the front path looking so upset that Noddy felt he couldn't sing his new song any more.

"I'll go and see Big-Ears," he thought as he put on his little hat with the jingling bell. "He might think it's a good idea to go away too. After all—I've

earned a lot of money this week, taking people to the station."

So Noddy jumped into his little car and drove away to Big-Ears' Toadstool House, hooting at naughty Martha Monkey who was playing with a ball in the middle of the road.

11

He soon came to Big-Ears' house and hooted outside merrily. "Parp-parp—parp-parp-parp!"

"Here I am, Noddy—hanging out my washing on the line!" called Big-Ears. "What's brought you here so early in the morning?"

"Oh, Big-Ears—I've thought of a new song—and a good idea too," said Noddy, jumping out of his car. "Listen!"

And first he sang his song which made Big-Ears clap loudly—and then he told him his idea.

"Big-Ears—everyone is going away—can't we go too? There soon won't be anyone left to take to the station!"

But Big-Ears shook his head at once. "No, Noddy. For one thing I've had to spend a lot of money on my brother Little-Ears, who has been ill—and for another *you* won't have much work to do for the next few weeks, so you'll have to save the money you've earned—not waste it on a holiday!"

NODDY SANG HIS SONG AND MADE
BIG-EARS CLAP LOUDLY

13

"Oh, Big-Ears—I do so want to go away!" said Noddy. "I'm tired of Toy Town. I want a change! Do, do let's go."

"No. We must be sensible," said Big-Ears.

"I don't like being sensible!" wailed Noddy. "It's a horrid thing to be. Let's be silly instead and go away!"

"Go away by yourself if you feel like that, Noddy," said Big-Ears, quite sternly, and will you believe it, he went into his Toadstool House and banged the door!

14

2. OFF TO CATCH THE TRAIN

NODDY was cross. He got into his car and banged the door shut with a very big slam indeed.

"Two people can play at banging doors!" he shouted, and drove off at top speed, almost running over Big-Ears' black cat. It sprang out of the way just in time.

"Why have we ALWAYS got to be sensible?" grumbled Noddy. "Everyone else is going away. *I* want to go too—oooh, that reminds me, I said I'd call for Sally Skittle and all her family at half-past nine. I shall be late! Hurry, car, hurry!"

The car raced along, almost knocked a lamp-post over and nearly bumped into Mr Plod, the policeman, who was crossing the road.

"Hey there!" shouted Mr Plod, angrily. "What do you think you're doing, Noddy?"

But Noddy had turned up the road to Sally Skittle's house, and jammed on his brakes so hard that his little car almost stood on its bonnet! He hooted loudly. "Parp-parp-parp!"

Sally Skittle came to the door. "Oh there you are, Noddy! You're late. I've sent some of the young skittles off already. Now then—can you take me, and three of the other skittles, and our luggage?"

Noddy jumped out of the car and ran to get the luggage. "Yes! You get in the front with me, Mrs Skittle. The others can go at the back. They'll have

16

to hold on to the luggage. Goodness, what a lot you've got! Look at all those buckets and spades!"

"We'll have to hurry," said Sally Skittle, and got into the car. "We don't want to miss the train, Noddy."

At last everyone was in. The little skittles were so excited that Noddy was sure they would fall out of the car before they got to the station.

"I can hear the train whistling, I can hear the train whistling!" cried little Sue Skittle, and gave Noddy a bang on the head with her spade. "Be quick, be quick!"

"You stop doing that!" said Noddy fiercely.

17

"I can't drive when people bang me on the head with spades. Oooh, she's done it again! Sally Skittle, tell her to stop!"

"You shouldn't have been late," said Sally Skittle. Then away they all went down the road and round the corner at sixty miles an hour!

"Parp-parp!" said the little car as it raced along, as excited as could be.

"Oooooh!" said Noddy, and put on the brakes. "There's Mr Plod again. Out of my way, Mr Plod, out of my way!" Parp-parp!

A bucket bounced out of the car and landed upside down on Mr Plod's helmet. The little skittles screamed in delight. Noddy didn't dare stop to pick up the bucket when he saw Mr Plod's angry, astonished face. He raced on down the road.

Mr Plod's roar followed him.

"NODDY! HAVE YOU GONE MAD? I'LL LOCK
YOU UP, I'LL . . ."

Noddy didn't hear any more, and swung into the
station yard just as the train was puffing into the
station. All the skittles tumbled out, snatched their
luggage and ran to the train, while Sally Skittle went
to get the tickets.

"I'll pay our taxi-fares when we get back again!"
cried Sally Skittle, hurrying to the train. "Oh, wait
for me, Guard, wait for me!"

"Well—they might have waved goodbye!" said
Noddy, as the train puffed out. "Oh dear—why did
that silly bucket have to land on Mr Plod's helmet.
I'd better be careful today and not go near him. He
didn't seem very pleased with me."

19

Noddy went off to look for some more toys to take in his little car. But Toy Town was very empty. Only Mr Wobbly Man wobbled down the street, and a little rabbit spun a top by himself in a corner.

"Good gracious! I shan't earn any money at all if the town is as empty as this," said little Noddy, nodding his head sadly. "I think Big-Ears is silly. We might just as well have gone away too!"

When Noddy went home for his dinner, he had a terrible shock. A notice was pinned to his door. This is what it said:

> TO LITTLE NODDY
> I WANT TO SEE YOU, SO COME
> TO THE POLICE STATION WITH
> YOUR LITTLE CAR
> —MR PLOD.

"Oh, my goodness!" said Noddy, in fright. "Now look at that! Well—I SHAN'T GO!"

3. MR MARVEL MONKEY

NODDY went indoors and cut himself some sandwiches, but he was so upset about the notice on his door that he couldn't eat them.

"I'd better go and tell Big-Ears," he said, his head nodding sadly. "He'll be cross again, but I simply *must* tell someone!"

He got into his little car and drove away. He wasn't looking out for passengers because he was sure there wouldn't be anyone. So he was most surprised to see a very well-dressed toy monkey standing on a corner, waving a tightly rolled green umbrella.

"Hi! Taxi!" shouted the monkey. Noddy stopped just by him.

"Do you want to go to the station?" asked Noddy, wondering who the monkey was. He was sure he had never seen him before. Perhaps he had been to stay with little Miss Monkey.

"No. I don't want to go to the station," said the monkey. "Let me introduce myself, taxi-man. I'm Mr Marvel Monkey, and I go about Toyland selling all kinds of things. I came here hoping to sell some of my goods, but dear me, how empty the town is!"

"Everyone's gone away," said Noddy. "What do you want me for, Mr Monkey, if you don't want to go to the station?"

"I used to go about on a bicycle with a little side-car for my big bag of goods," said Mr Monkey. "But it broke down yesterday and will take two weeks to be mended. So I wondered if I could hire you to take me on my travels? I'll pay you very, very well."

"Oh—that sounds exciting!" said Noddy. "I've been longing to go away for a holiday—and that would be *like* a holiday for me, wouldn't it, Mr Monkey?"

"Of course, of course!" said Mr Monkey, smiling broadly. "You look a very nice little fellow, and I know you can drive fast. I saw you almost knock over that horrid policeman this morning. Ha ha—I did laugh!"

"Well, he *is* being rather horrid today," said Noddy. "He pinned a notice to my door to say I was to go and see him tonight—but if I do he'll lock me up, I'm sure."

"Of course he will!" said Mr Monkey. "So that's another reason why you should come away with me in your little car. By the time you come back that policeman will have forgotten about the notice."

"Well—I don't know about that," said Noddy.

23

"Where are you going to, Mr Monkey? And what do you sell?"

"Oh—all kinds of things," said Mr Monkey. "And I want to go to all kinds of places—Rocking-Horse Town, Clockwork-Clown Village, Toy-Dog Town— ah, we'll go all over the place! I like you, little nodding man. Will you come?"

"I'd love to," said Noddy, and his head nodded fast. "But wait a minute—I'll have to go to my friend Big-Ears the brownie first, and ask him to take the key of my house and look after it while I'm away."

"Very well," said Mr Monkey. "Let's go and see him. I'll get into your car, and put my bag at the back."

So away went Mr Marvel Monkey and Noddy, down the road, up the hill and through the wood, hooting at the little rabbits playing there.

"I wonder if Big-Ears is still cross with me?"

thought Noddy. "Ah— here's his house. I'll hoot."

"Parp-parp-parp!" said the car, and Big-Ears looked out of his window at once.

24

"PARP-PARP-PARP!" SAID THE CAR, AND BIG-EARS
LOOKED OUT OF HIS WINDOW AT ONCE

"Oh—it's you, little Noddy," he said. "Who is that with you?"

"Big-Ears, I've got something VERY exciting to tell you!" said Noddy. "Can I come in for a moment? I'm going away and I want to ask you to take the key of my little House-For-One."

"Going *away!*" said Big-Ears. "But I told you *not* to. And please tell me who that is you've got in your car."

"You still sound cross," said Noddy. He got out of the car, and Mr Monkey got out too. They both went into Big-Ears' house.

"So VERY pleased to meet you, Mr Big-Ears," said Mr Monkey, and shook hands with Big-Ears for so long that the brownie had to drag his hand away. "Any friend of little Noddy is a friend of mine!"

"Hm!" said Big-Ears, not looking at all friendly. "Sit down. Now, Noddy, what *is* this about? Please tell me at once."

26

4. OFF TO ROCKING-HORSE TOWN

SO Noddy told Big-Ears all about Mr Plod's notice on his door, and then about Mr Monkey wanting to hire his car to go travelling.

"You see, I *do* want a holiday, Big-Ears, and this would be a lovely change for me," said Noddy, nodding his head so fast that it made Big-Ears' cat quite giddy to look at him. "And I DON'T want to go and see Mr Plod tonight."

"Well, you *ought* to go," said Big-Ears. "He probably only wants to scold you, and I must say you sound as if you deserve it. And what is the name of this monkey? You haven't told me yet."

"It's Mr Marvel Monkey," said Noddy.

"What a peculiar name!" said Big-Ears, staring at Mr Monkey. "*Marvel* Monkey!"

"It's short for Marvellous," said Mr Monkey, smiling in a most friendly fashion at Big-Ears. "I can do all sorts of marvellous things—both big *and* small. Like this, for instance!" And to Noddy's astonishment Mr Monkey's tail came slipping out from behind him and snatched Big-Ears' red hat off his head!

Noddy laughed loudly, but Big-Ears didn't even smile. He snatched back his hat. "*That's* not marvellous, it's just bad manners!" he said. "Go away, please. You wouldn't be good for Noddy."

"Oh, but surely it's for *Noddy* to say if he'll take me round in his car or not," said Mr Monkey, still smiling. "Isn't it, little Noddy? This

friend of yours seems very cross. Shall we go?"

"Yes," said Noddy. "I do so want a little holiday.
You come too, Big-Ears!"

"What—come with a monkey like that!" said Big-
Ears. "Certainly not. We don't know anything about
him. And I don't think you ought to go either,
Noddy."

Mr Monkey stood up, bowed very politely to
Big-Ears and walked to the door. "Goodbye," he
said. "So pleased to have met you!" And dear me,
that tail of his stretched itself out and took Big-
Ears' handkerchief out of his pocket!

Noddy followed Mr Monkey, feeling excited.
Bother Big-Ears! He would go with Mr Monkey
and have some fun with him—and earn a lot of
money!

"Goodbye, Big-Ears," said Noddy, but Big-Ears

29

didn't even look at him. Oh dear—he *was* cross! Noddy gave a big sigh and went to his car.

"Come on, Mr Monkey," he said. "Where do you want me to go first?"

"Er—let me see now—to Rocking-Horse Town, I think," said Mr Monkey, settling himself beside Noddy in the car. "I've got some beautiful new horse tails to sell there. Off we go!"

And off they went, and a funny little song came into Noddy's head as the car bumped through the wood.

"Off we go
   To Rocking-Horse Town
   Where every horse
   Goes up and down
   With a long, long tail
   And a neigh, neigh,
      neigh,
   We'll see them all
   Go rocking away!"

Mr Monkey patted Noddy
on the back. "What a wonderful song!" he said.
"You *are* a clever little fellow. We shall be great
friends, I can tell. Sing your song again!"

Noddy felt very proud indeed, and his head
nodded very fast. Really, Mr Monkey *was* nice! He
sang the song all over again at the top of his voice
and Mr Monkey joined in.

Soon they came to Rocking-Horse Town, and
met all kinds of rocking-horses on the road, some
big, some quite small. Mr Monkey greeted them all!

"Hallo there! Do you want a brand-new tail?"

"Nay, nay, nay!" said the horses and rocked away
fast.

"Can't they say anything? Do they neigh all the
time?" said Mr Monkey.

31

"They weren't neighing then. They were saying 'Nay' and that means 'No'," said Noddy. "I'm afraid you won't sell your tails here, Mr Monkey. All the tails I saw were very fine ones."

"Ah well—you never know," said Mr Monkey. "We will stop here for the night. Can you sleep in your car? I have a little tent I put up for myself each night, but it only takes one person."

"Oh yes—I can easily cuddle up on my front seat with a rug," said Noddy. "It's nice warm weather. But it isn't evening yet. Let's go round the town."

So they had a nice walk round Rocking-Horse Town, and had a meal in a little shop. Mr Monkey tried to sell some tails, but it wasn't any good

None of the rocking-horses wanted one.

"Nay, nay, nay!" they said, just as before.

"Well, well—we can't always be lucky," said Mr Monkey. "Now let's settle down for the night beside the car. Look, I'm going to put up my little tent. If you feel lonely in the night, little Noddy, just look at my tent and you'll see my tail curling out from underneath it — just to keep you company!"

"Oh, thank you!" said Noddy. "I *might* feel a bit scared, being away from home. If I am, I'll just peep out of my car and see your tail, and I'll know you're nearby. Good night, Mr Monkey. We're going to have some fun, aren't we?"

"We certainly are!" said Mr Monkey, and went into his tent. He pushed his long tail outside where Noddy could see it, and waggled it at him. "Good night—sleep well!"

5. TAILS FOR SALE!

NODDY cuddled up in the front seat of his little car and pulled the rug round him. He soon went to sleep. An owl woke him in the middle of the night and frightened him.

"Hoo!" said the owl. "Hoo-hoo-hoo!"

"What's that? Who is hooing at me?" said Noddy, sitting up. "Where am I? I'm scared! Oh, of course—I'm with Mr Marvel Monkey. Shall I call out to him and tell him I'm scared?"

He called softly, "Mr Monkey! I'm scared!" But nobody answered. Was Mr Monkey there? Noddy peeped over at the tent. In the bright moonlight he saw Mr Monkey's tail poking out from underneath it.

"Oh well—I'd better not wake him!" said Noddy. "He thinks I'm very, very clever, and he might change his mind if he knew I was frightened. I'll look at his tail for a minute or two, then I'll feel better."

It wasn't long before Noddy was asleep again, and he didn't wake up till Mr Monkey tapped him on the shoulder.

"Noddy! Wake up! We're going to be very busy!"

Noddy sat up in surprise. Busy? What did Mr

Monkey mean? Then, to his astonishment, he saw seven rocking-horses rocking all round them!

"Oh—what have *you* come for?" said Noddy, nodding his head up and down in delight. "I do like you. You have such nice faces, rocking-horses."

The rocking-horses neighed loudly, and then turned their backs on Noddy and Mr Monkey—and Noddy had such a shock! They had no tails!

"They've come to buy new tails," said Mr Monkey. "They lost theirs last night. What a bit of luck for us, Noddy!"

"Goodness—but however did they lose them?" said Noddy, astonished. "How careless rocking-horses must be!"

"Nay, nay!" said a big black and white horse rocking round Noddy.

"Noddy—take these tails," said Mr Monkey, handing him seven fine ones out of his bag. "Hold each one while I dab glue on one end—and then fit them on to the horses."

Noddy did as he was told. He went to the first horse and gave a little cry. "Oh, what a shame— your tail has been *cut* off, rocking-horse. Didn't you know?"

36

NODDY HELD THE TAILS WHILST MR MONKEY
DABBED GLUE ON THEM

37

"Nay, nay!" said the horse in surprise, and tried to look round at his tail. But he couldn't quite manage it. Noddy stuck the new tail on very carefully, just above what was left of the old tail.

Then he went to the next horse—and, dear me, that one's tail had been cut off too—in fact the same thing had happened to ALL the rocking-horses! How very astonishing!

"How did it happen, do you suppose, Mr Monkey?" asked Noddy. Mr Monkey shook his head.

"Who knows? Anyway, it was *very* lucky for them that we were here this morning with new tails in our bag! Now, rocking-horses—that is a shilling for each tail, please."

Mr Monkey put all the money into his pocket, looking pleased. "Now we will go on to Clockwork-Clown Village," he said. "Drive off, please, Noddy. We've done well here."

So away went Noddy and Mr Monkey in the little car again. Mr Monkey bought some breakfast for them both and they ate it in the car.

"This really is *fun*," said Noddy. "Ah, look—there's a sign-post for Clockwork-Clown Village!"

38

6. CLOCKWORK-CLOWN VILLAGE

NODDY sang as they went, and Mr Monkey's tail came out from under him and beat time.

"The clockwork clowns
Go clickity-clack.
You wind them up
At the back, back, back!
Then head-over-heels
You'll see them go,
Clickity-clack,
In a rollicking row!
Oh clickity-clack and clackity-click,
I wish I could do such a comical trick!"

Noddy shouted out the last word and Mr Monkey beamed at him.

"Very, very clever," he said. "I shall have

to pay you double money, I can see—half for your work, and half for your songs. Wonderful, really wonderful!"

Noddy went pink with delight. How very, very nice Mr Monkey was! MUCH nicer than cross old Big-Ears.

Soon they drove into Clockwork-Clown Village. Clowns were all over the place, turning head-

over-heels, walking on their hands, and running about with the clickity-click sound made by their clockwork. It really was fun to see them.

"Stop in the market-place," said Mr Monkey.

"I have something to call out there." So Noddy stopped when he came to the busy little market-place, where all kinds of clowns were buying and selling.

Mr Monkey stood up in the car and began to shout. "Keys for sale! Buy one in case you lose yours! Keys for sale, strong and new and bright!"

But nobody came to buy. One clown took his key out of his back and waggled it under Mr Monkey's nose.

"*We* don't lose our keys! I've had mine for fifteen years! You won't find much trade here, Monkey!"

"I think he's right, Mr Monkey," said Noddy. "Every single clown has a key. We'd better go on to the next village."

"No. We'll stay here for a night," said Mr Monkey. "I want to buy a few things at the market. Besides— you never know what will happen. We *might* sell a few keys!"

So they spent the day at the market, and Noddy really enjoyed it. He had plenty of money with

him, for he had brought all that he had earned during the last two weeks. He bought quite a lot of things.

"Dear me—you seem very rich!" said Mr Monkey in surprise. "Who is that lovely little sash for?"

"For a friend of mine—little Tessie Bear," said Noddy. "And look—this is for dear Mrs Tubby—do you think she will like it?"

He held out a hat with flowers on. Mr Monkey laughed, took off his own hat, and put on the one Noddy had bought. He looked very funny in it and Noddy laughed too.

The day went quickly, and soon it was time to camp out again. Mr Monkey found a little backyard and put up his tent. Noddy curled up in the front seat of the car, quite tired out. He fell asleep at once.

Something woke him in the middle of the night. What was it? Someone was shouting! Oh dear—what was happening? Had Mr Monkey heard it? Noddy looked over at the little tent.

No, Mr Monkey couldn't have heard it. There was his long brown tail peeping out from under the tent just as before. Noddy settled down again, feeling glad that Mr Monkey was close by.

In the morning Mr Monkey folded up his tent, put it in the back of the car with his bag, and

Noddy drove out of the little yard into the main street.

As soon as the clockwork clowns saw the car, they surrounded it at once! Noddy was very surprised.

"Hey! Have you got any keys left?" cried one. "My brother had his stolen in the night! He must have another, or he can't be wound up!"

"And both of my friends have had theirs

43

taken!" cried another clown. "I want two keys!"

"Dear dear!" said Mr Monkey, in a most surprised voice. "What a good thing we spent the night here!"

"I *thought* I heard someone shouting in the night!" said little Noddy.

"Yes—they all shouted when they found their keys had been stolen!" said the first clown. "Hey, Monkey, how much are your keys?"

"Two shillings each," said Mr Monkey, and took some out of his bag. "Very cheap. Shining bright!"

"Cheap! Why, they ought to be a *penny* each!" said a clown fiercely. Mr Monkey at once put his keys back into his bag.

"I only sell GOOD keys," he said. "Noddy, drive on."

"No, wait—wait!" said the clown. "We've *got* to have the keys. All right—we'll pay."

Then out came the keys from the bag again, and Mr Monkey took a great deal of money. He beamed all round.

"Well, goodbye! I *am* so glad I was able to do you clowns a good turn. Off we go, Noddy."

Off they went down the road, with Mr Monkey humming gaily. "*What* a bit of luck!" he said. "I really am a lucky fellow."

"I think you are, too," said Noddy. "Where are we going now, Mr Monkey?"

"Toy-Dog Town," said Mr Monkey. "I've some whiskers to sell there. Toy dogs are very proud of their whiskers, you know, Noddy."

"Yes, I know," said Noddy. "So are toy cats. Miss Fluffy Cat has wonderful whiskers. Ah—here is the road for Toy-Dog Town. Well—let's hope we are lucky there too!"

45

7. TOY-DOG TOWN

TOY-DOG Town was quite a small place. It was full of toy dogs of all kinds and sizes and shapes, some with bows round their necks, some with ribbons on their tails, some with pretty little jackets.

They ran round the car, wagging their tails. Mr Monkey's tail came curling out of the car, and shook the paws of the nearby dogs. Noddy thought it was very funny. He looked at their whiskers.

"They've all got very fine whiskers," he

46

whispered to Mr Monkey. "It's no good staying here!"

"We'll try our luck," said Mr Monkey, and stood up in the car to shout. "Whiskers for sale! Very long fine ones, that will last for ever! Black, white, brown, grey—or if you want the latest fashion—green!"

But nobody wanted the latest fashion. "*Green* whiskers," said a pretty little poodle, turning up her small black nose. "What an idea!"

"You might be glad of them if you hadn't any whiskers at all!" called Mr Monkey. He turned to Noddy. "Oh well—we'll spend the day here. I've an old friend, Mr Puggy Dog. I'll go and see him. You have a look round."

Noddy was rather bored that day. He thought of Big-Ears and wondered if he was still cross with him. He thought of his little House-For-One, and kind Mrs Tubby Bear.

He wandered down a little street, all alone, and then, round a corner, he came across a small toy puppy-dog, crying all by herself. She was black and white, with a little pink nose and tongue, and a pink ribbon round her neck.

47

"What's the matter?" said Noddy, sitting down beside the tiny thing. "Why—you haven't any whiskers! At least—only two!"

"I know. That's why I'm crying," said the puppy-dog. "The toy puppy-dog next door fought me, and bit off nearly all my lovely black whiskers."

"Well don't cry any more," said Noddy. "*I* can help you! My friend and I *sell* whiskers! Come back to my little car, and I'll get you some."

So off they went to Noddy's car, and Noddy looked for Mr Monkey's bag. Ah—there it was, under the packed-up tent. He pulled it out. It was locked, but Noddy knew where Mr Monkey kept the key—hidden under the seat of the car.

He unlocked the bag and began to look for the whiskers—and then he sat down suddenly and stared into the bag as if he couldn't believe his eyes!

"Why—there are old rocking-horse tails here—*cut-off ones!*" he said. "And my goodness—look at these old clockwork keys! And here's a big pair of scissors—what are they for? Aha—I can guess! They're for cutting off rocking-horse tails—and dogs' WHISKERS! OH! I can't believe it!"

"HERE'S A BIG PAIR OF SCISSORS!" EXCLAIMED NODDY
TO THE LITTLE PUPPY-DOG

49

Then Noddy found something else. "And look at this —a monkey's tail! Now why does he keep *that* here? Oh, *I* know! It's the one he . . ."

"Please—are there any whiskers to fit me?" asked the little puppy-dog.

"Yes—choose which you like—and you don't need to pay for them!" said Noddy. So the little puppy chose a packet of long black whiskers, gave Noddy a grateful lick on his nose, and ran off happily.

Just as she left, who should come up but Mr Monkey, beaming all over his face as usual.

"Noddy," he began, "do you know you didn't sing me a song about Toy-Dog Town? Now, wouldn't you like . . .?"

"Mr Monkey! Look what I've found in your bag!" cried Noddy, fiercely. "You're a fraud! You're wicked! You're . . ."

50

"How DARE you open my bag!" said Mr Monkey, looking very angry indeed. "I'll report you to the police. I won't pay you a penny! I'll . . ."

"You stole out in the night and cut off the rocking-horses' tails!" said Noddy. "You went out the next night and stole the clockwork clowns' keys. You did, you did! And tonight you were going to cut off the toy dogs' whiskers—yes, and leave

your horrid tail outside the tent to make me think you were asleep all the time!"

"How *could* I leave my tail outside if I went off to steal keys?" shouted Mr Monkey angrily.

"You left this *old* tail sticking out under your tent!" cried Noddy, and smacked Mr Monkey with it. "I'm going to take you to Toy Town and tell Mr Plod about you."

And what do you think Noddy did? He pushed Mr Monkey over, sat down very hard on him, and tied his wrists together with his old tail! Then he dragged him to the car by his real tail, and sat him in the front seat.

"I'll jump out! I'll fight you! I'll run away!" shouted Mr Monkey.

"You won't," said Noddy. "I'm going to sit down hard on your tail, Mr Monkey—so if you jump out, you'll leave your beautiful long tail behind—and nobody's going to sell *you* another!"

And away they went at top speed back to Toy Town. Well, well, well—who would have thought such a thing would happen!

8. SURPRISE FOR MR PLOD!

NODDY drove all the way home sitting on Mr Monkey's tail. He felt very angry, very fierce, and very upset.

"To think that *I* should have helped this horrid monkey to deceive everyone!" he thought. "Oh, Big-Ears was right. He's always right. Oh dear, will he ever forgive me for disobeying him and getting into this dreadful fix? Mr Plod may put *me* in prison too, for going off with a bad monkey."

Noddy came to Toy Town. He drove right past his own little house and was glad to see that Mr Plod's notice was no longer pinned to his front door. Then he went on to the police-station. He didn't get out because he was still sitting on Mr Monkey's tail.

"I know quite well that the minute I get up you'll be off!" he said to the monkey. "So I'll just sit here and HOOT!"

He hooted loudly. "PARP-PARP-PARP-PARP-PARP!" Mr Plod came rushing out at once.

"Now, now—what's all this? Good gracious it's

you, little Noddy! Wherever have you been? Hey, Big-Ears, here's Noddy back again!"

And out came Big-Ears too. He pointed at Mr Monkey at once. "There's that monkey —the one you said

you wanted, Mr Plod!" he said. "The one you've had all kinds of complaints about. Noddy, how *dare* you go off with that monkey? He's bad, he's . . ."

"Yes," said Noddy. "I found that out, so I've brought him to Mr Plod—*oh*, the things he . . ."

"We know *everything* about him," said Mr Plod, pointing to a big notice on the police-station wall. "Look, there's his picture. WANTED,

54

MR PLOD POINTED TO A BIG NOTICE ON THE
POLICE-STATION WALL

MR MARVEL MONKEY. ANYONE GIVING INFORMATION ABOUT THIS RASCAL WILL GET A BIG REWARD."

"Good gracious!" said Noddy. "A big reward! Well, here he is. I can't get up, I'm sitting on his tail to make sure he doesn't jump out. Can you get hold of him please, Mr Plod?"

Mr Plod jerked Mr Monkey out of the car, and took him by the arm, and Noddy followed, holding his tail. Aha! Mr Marvel Monkey was well and truly caught!

Mr Plod put him into a cell and locked the door. Mr Monkey yelled and banged on the door, but it wasn't a bit of good. Nobody took any notice at all.

"Mr Plod—I know I oughtn't to have gone off

with that bad monkey," said Noddy. "Big-Ears told me not to. But it's a good thing I did, isn't it, because I found out his wicked tricks—and brought him back to you!"

"Yes—it's turned out better than you deserve, Noddy," said Mr Plod. "Didn't you see that notice on your door before you left? I wanted you to come and see me that night and you didn't come."

"I know. I was afraid to," said Noddy. "I thought you were going to scold me. Wasn't that what the notice was for?"

"No. It was just to tell you to look out for Mr Monkey," said Mr Plod. "You see, you get about in your little car and see a lot of people—and when I heard about that wicked monkey coming to our town, I thought I would have a word with you, and get you to look out for him. But you didn't come and see me."

"Oh dear! What a pity!" said Noddy. "I wouldn't have gone away with Mr Monkey then—and all those horrid things wouldn't have happened."

"Still—everything has turned out well," said Big-Ears, giving Noddy his kindest smile. "I'm sorry I was so cross with you, Noddy—but you *are* a little turnip-head sometimes, you know! And I *didn't* like the way that Mr Monkey snatched off my hat with his tail. So very rude."

Noddy ran to Big-Ears and gave him a hug. "I won't be a turnip-head any more!" he said. "I missed you while I was away, Big-Ears. I did really!"

"Well now," said Mr Plod, "why don't you two go away for a little holiday, and forget all about this? Everyone's on holiday now—except poor old Plod!"

"Let's all three go!" said Big-Ears. "You really *do* need a holiday too, Mr Plod!"

"I can't leave my job," said Mr Plod, shaking his head sadly.

"I can't go either," said Noddy. "I spent all my money in the market at Clockwork-Clown Village. Oh dear—and I can't earn any more because everybody's away."

"You forget, Noddy—there's a BIG reward

offered for Mr Monkey's capture," said Mr Plod, beaming all over his face. "Why don't you spend *that* money? I'll go and get it now."

And away he went—and came back with a large purse of money. "Here you are," he said. "Now go and enjoy yourselves—and send me a nice post-card as soon as you get to the seaside!"

Well! What a wonderful thing! Noddy took hold of Big-Ears and danced him round and round until his red hat fell off.

"Let's go now, this very minute!" cried Noddy. "Quickly! Before you change your mind and want to be sensible, Big-Ears! Goodbye, Mr Plod. Come along, Big-Ears, come along!"

And goodness me, look, away they go at top speed in Noddy's little car, waving to Mr Plod. Noddy is singing very loudly indeed. What is he singing? Perhaps you can guess!

"The sun is shining
Up in the sky,
The birds are singing,
And so am I!
The bees are buzzing
As loud as can be,
The flowers are nodding
Their heads, like me!
The wind is blowing
The clouds along,
And I am singing
My little song!"

Goodbye, Noddy and Big-Ears. Have a lovely time. We'll see you again soon.